R.L.

S0-FDQ-898

WITHDRAWN

Property of
Boone County Library
Harrison, Arkansas

ANIMAL RIGHTS

CAPTIVE ANIMAL WELFARE

Jessie Alkire

Checkerboard Library

An Imprint of Abdo Publishing
abdopublishing.com

abdopublishing.com

Published by Abdo Publishing, a division of ABDO, PO Box 398166, Minneapolis, Minnesota 55439. Copyright © 2018 by Abdo Consulting Group, Inc. International copyrights reserved in all countries. No part of this book may be reproduced in any form without written permission from the publisher. Checkerboard Library™ is a trademark and logo of Abdo Publishing.

Printed in the United States of America, North Mankato, Minnesota
102017
012018

Design: Christa Schneider, Mighty Media, Inc.
Production: Mighty Media, Inc.
Editor: Megan Borgert-Spaniol
Cover Photographs: Shutterstock
Interior Photographs: Alamy, pp. 15, 23, 27; iStockphoto, pp. 11, 19, 28 (bottom), 29 (left); Shutterstock, pp. 4 (left, middle, right), 5, 10, 13, 17, 21, 22, 25, 28 (top, middle), 29 (right); Wikimedia Commons, pp. 7, 9

Publisher's Cataloging-in-Publication Data
Names: Alkire, Jessie, author.
Title: Captive animal welfare / by Jessie Alkire.
Description: Minneapolis, Minnesota : Abdo Publishing, 2018. | Series: Animal rights | Includes online resources and index.
Identifiers: LCCN 2017944021 | ISBN 9781532112584 (lib.bdg.) | ISBN 9781532150302 (ebook)
Subjects: LCSH: Zoo animals--Juvenile literature. | Animal rights movement--Juvenile literature. | Animal welfare--Juvenile literature.
Classification: DDC 590.73--dc23
LC record available at https://lccn.loc.gov/2017944021

CONTENTS

- What Are Captive Animals? ... 4
- Ancient Animal Collections ... 6
- Animal Museums ... 8
- The Modern Zoo ... 10
- Marine Parks ... 12
- Education & Conservation ... 14
- Captive Animal Issues & Ethics ... 16
- The Captive Animal Movement ... 18
- Laws & Regulations ... 20
- Rescuing Captive Animals ... 22
- Captive Animal Alternatives ... 24
- The Future of Animal Captivity ... 26
- Timeline ... 28
- Become an Animal Advocate ... 29
- Glossary ... 30
- Online Resources ... 31
- Index ... 32

WHAT ARE CAPTIVE ANIMALS?

Have you ever observed wild animals at a zoo or aquarium? Maybe you watched the animals as they moved around in cages or small enclosures. These animals are not free as they would be in the wild. They are captive animals.

Captive animals are wild animals that are **confined** and cared for by humans. Some captive animals are taken from the wild and put into captivity. Others are born into captivity.

Common captive animals include tigers, elephants, monkeys, and dolphins. Some captive animals are personal pets. Most are housed in zoos, aquariums, circuses, and other places of entertainment.

Animal captivity is **controversial**. Animal rights **advocates** believe it is **unethical** to keep wild animals in captivity. The animals are confined to limited spaces. They don't get to live as they would in their natural **habitats**. Animal advocates have brought increased attention to the issue of captive animal welfare. Today, public pressure and advancements in **technology** play important roles in improving the well-being of captive animals.

ANCIENT ANIMAL COLLECTIONS

The history of captive animals dates to ancient times. The first zoos were created in 2500 BCE in Egypt and Mesopotamia. These zoos were not the kind that anyone could visit. They were private collections of wild animals called menageries.

Menageries were symbols of power and wealth. Historical records suggest menagerie owners sent hunters far and wide to bring back animals. These animals included giraffes, elephants, birds, bears, and more.

Other menageries existed later in China, Greece, Italy, and what is now Mexico. In the 1500s, Aztec ruler Montezuma had one of the largest animal collections of all time. His menagerie was full of mammals, birds, reptiles, and fish.

Traveling menageries became popular in the 1700s. Owners displayed their wild animal collections for the public.

Wild animals were also made to fight in public. Fifteen hundred years ago, ancient Romans would release the animals into large arenas. Huge crowds gathered to watch the animals fight one another and with human fighters called gladiators.

Historians believe these Roman animal fights were some of the first circuses. The modern circus developed hundreds of years later. Animals such as elephants, lions, and tigers were trained to perform tricks in front of crowds.

ANIMAL MUSEUMS

The first public zoos began to appear in Europe in the late 1700s. This was during the Age of Enlightenment. This period in Europe was marked by a movement that placed increased value on discovery and reason. Zoos came about because scientists wanted to study animals in captivity.

One of the first public zoos was built in Paris, France, in 1793. It was named the Ménagerie du Jardin des Plantes. The zoo still exists today! Many other zoos followed in the United Kingdom, Canada, and the United States in the 1800s.

These early public zoos were like museums. Their animals were meant to be observed and studied. The zoos were often low cost or free to encourage public education. Owners tried to house as many animals as possible. The animals were kept in small spaces or cages. Such conditions did not promote the comfort or welfare of the animals.

In the 1900s, zoos shifted toward more natural **environments**. In 1907, German animal trainer Carl Hagenbeck opened the world's first zoo without traditional cages. He tried to recreate animals' natural **habitats**. The animals were separated from onlookers by channels of water.

With Hagenbeck's design, zoo visitors could not get as close to animals. But the natural settings gave the animals more space. This was better for the animals' well-being than cages were. Other zoos later adopted Hagenbeck's ideas and made similar enclosures.

The word *zoo* comes from "zoological garden." But early zoos kept animals in cement and iron cages, not gardens.

THE MODERN ZOO

In 1924, the Association of Zoos and Aquariums (AZA) was founded. This organization sets standards for zoos and aquariums in the United States and several other countries. These standards focus on the care and living conditions of zoo animals. They also encourage **donations** to or participation in conservation efforts. Facilities that meet these standards are **accredited** by the AZA.

There are more than 200 AZA-accredited zoos and aquariums in the United States. One is the San Diego Zoo in California. This 100-acre (40 ha) park is the largest zoo in the United States. It houses more than 4,000 animals. The zoo also works to breed **endangered** animals in captivity and return them back to the wild.

AZA-accredited zoos give their animals space and comfortable living conditions. They try to create an **environment** similar to what animals would experience in the wild.

Endangered aquatic box turtle

Most zoos in the United States are not **accredited** by the AZA. Many of these are smaller zoos, including roadside and petting zoos. Their animals may live in extreme conditions, from small indoor cages to concrete enclosures with little shade. They may have little if any interaction with other members of their species.

But even AZA-accredited zoos have their limits. Their natural settings cannot provide the same freedom of the wild. They do not allow the animals to roam, fly, hunt, or mate as they naturally would.

Many modern zoo exhibits are inspired by where the animals come from. These exhibits teach visitors about the animals' natural habitats.

MARINE PARKS

As modern zoos developed, they began to include aquariums. The first aquarium opened in 1853 at the London Zoo in England. More aquariums and marine animal exhibits soon opened at other zoos. In 1938, Marine Studios opened in Florida. It was the first facility devoted entirely to marine animals. Marine Studios put on shows in which dolphins, whales, and other animals did tricks.

The popularity of marine parks increased with the 1963 release of the film *Flipper*. The movie is about a boy who becomes friends with a dolphin. The next year, popular marine park SeaWorld opened in San Diego, California. It was the first marine park to have an orca, or killer whale. SeaWorld soon began to breed orcas in captivity.

Today's marine parks commonly house dolphins, whales, sea lions, and seals. Like zoos, not all marine parks are **accredited**. But even accredited parks cannot recreate life in the wild.

The Alliance of Marine Mammal Parks and Aquariums is similar to the AZA. Marine parks, aquariums, and zoos must meet its standards to be accredited.

At marine parks, animals built for swimming miles a day are kept in cement aquariums or pools. Trainers teach them to perform tricks for large audiences. Visitors are sometimes invited to pet, feed, or even swim with the marine animals. Such human interaction invades the animals' already limited space.

EDUCATION & CONSERVATION

Zoos and marine parks have goals besides entertainment. They also want to educate people. Visitors can observe the animals up close and learn about them. Researchers can also study the animals in captivity in a way that isn't possible in the wild.

Another main goal of zoos and marine parks is conservation. Many wild animals are threatened by **habitat** loss, lack of food, and illegal hunting. Some species are **endangered** in the wild.

Rehabilitating endangered species is one aspect of conservation. In the 1980s, about 30 California condors were left in the world. Then, the San Diego Wild Animal Park and Los Angeles Zoo started capturing these birds. The condors were bred in captivity and then released into the wild.

Zoos and marine parks also **rehabilitate** sick, injured, or orphaned animals. Bears, sea lions, otters, and walruses are commonly rescued animals. Some of these animals are released back into the wild. If they will not survive in the wild, they are kept in captivity.

The total number of California condors has increased since the 1980s. In 2016, there were nearly 450 California condors in the world!

CAPTIVE ANIMAL ISSUES & ETHICS

Zoos and marine parks offer many educational and conservation benefits. But remember, they cannot give animals the same freedom of their natural **habitats**. Also, captive animals often endure both mental and physical harm. Because of this, animal rights groups believe keeping animals in captivity is **unethical**.

In captivity, wild animals experience boredom and mental distress. They often display these emotions by pacing, walking in circles, or becoming **aggressive**. This can lead to **disaster**. For example, captive orcas have attacked and even killed their trainers. No orca in the wild has ever killed a human.

Captivity can also harm animals physically. For example, elephants need wide open spaces and soft ground to walk on.

Orcas can swim 100 miles (161 km) per day in the wild. Captive orcas experience collapsed fins from lack of exercise.

Many zoos cannot provide this kind of **habitat**. As a result, many captive elephants have died due to foot conditions.

For these reasons, animal rights groups believe wild animals are unfit for **confinement**. They also argue that **rehabilitation** efforts are not helpful if the animals cannot return to the wild. Animal **advocates** believe zoos and marine parks should contribute more to habitat conservation. This includes **donating** more of their incomes to preventing habitat loss and illegal hunting.

THE CAPTIVE ANIMAL MOVEMENT

The issues and **ethics** of animal captivity have led to a growing movement against it. In 1980, People for the Ethical Treatment of Animals (PETA) was founded. PETA took a firm position against using animals for entertainment. Organizations like this have since fought for policies that protect the well-being of captive animals.

The biggest changes in animal captivity have occurred in circuses. In the 1980s and 1990s, PETA and other groups helped expose animal mistreatment in circuses. Cities worldwide began to ban this entertainment. Many circuses have closed as a result.

It has taken longer for the movement against zoos and marine parks to gain support. Going to zoos and marine parks is an enjoyable tradition for many people. But public opinion began to shift after the release of *Blackfish* in 2013. This film is about an orca that was involved in the deaths of three people. The deaths occurred at the marine parks SeaWorld and Sealand of the Pacific. Some believe the orca's behavior resulted from living in captivity.

Many people have since protested SeaWorld and other marine parks. In 2015, SeaWorld promised to **donate** $10 million to wild orca research and conservation. In 2016, the company also announced the end of its orca breeding program.

In July 2013, animal advocates gathered in San Diego for an international protest to raise awareness of animal captivity in marine parks.

LAWS & REGULATIONS

The captive animal welfare movement has led to laws that protect captive animals. The 1966 Animal Welfare Act (AWA) regulates the housing and care of captive animals in the United States. But it does not include certain animals, such as fish and reptiles.

The AWA requires that animals be fed, watered, and given shelter. Animal **advocates** believe these standards should be higher. For example, a cement enclosure with room for movement would meet AWA standards. But animal advocates feel such a space is not **stimulating** enough for a wild animal.

Marine animals have little legal protection in the United States. The Marine Mammal Protection Act forbids capturing wild orcas without a permit. However, a permit allows the capture of orcas

The AWA does not protect the mental health of captive animals other than primates.

for research or entertainment. This means marine parks can legally take animals from the wild.

Some US states and other countries have passed stricter laws. South Carolina, New York, and California have banned keeping orcas and other marine animals in captivity. Costa Rica has closed its zoos and banned the capture of marine animals. The United Kingdom and many other countries have banned captive dolphins. And since 2009, India has banned keeping elephants in captivity.

RESCUING CAPTIVE ANIMALS

When laws are passed banning captivity of certain animals, animals already in captivity usually cannot be returned to the wild. Most don't have the survival skills to hunt prey or escape predators in the wild. The animals are often moved to wildlife refuges called **sanctuaries**. In sanctuaries, animals have more space and freedom than they would in zoos. However, sanctuaries can still exhibit their animals to the public as zoos do.

For retiring marine animals, some **advocates** promote sea pens. These ocean enclosures are surrounded by netting. The animals can swim, dive, and interact with ocean animals. However, sea pens may expose captive animals to ocean toxins, viruses, and weather conditions they cannot handle.

RIGHTS SPOTLIGHT

THE ELEPHANT SANCTUARY

The Elephant Sanctuary is a Tennessee organization founded in 1995. It provides refuge to elephants retired from zoos and circuses. The 2,700-acre (1,093 ha) habitat allows elephants to roam and interact with one another. Old and sick elephants receive veterinary care.

Tarra is an elephant at the Elephant Sanctuary. She was best friends with Bella the dog until Bella's death in 2011.

The sanctuary features a public education center where people can learn about Asian and African elephants. The organization also works with other elephant welfare groups to raise awareness. The Elephant Sanctuary is closed to the public, but viewers can still see the elephants by webcam!

CAPTIVE ANIMAL ALTERNATIVES

The captive animal welfare movement continues to gain support. It has led to exploration of **alternatives** to traditional zoos and marine parks. These alternatives allow humans to observe animals without invading their natural **habitats**.

One alternative is webcams. Several **sanctuaries** use this **technology** to allow people to watch live streams of captive animals. Explore.org has even partnered with conservation groups and national parks to place webcams in the wild. The website hosts a variety of live streams that feature animals from tigers to puffins.

Another alternative is virtual reality. Virtual reality is an artificial **environment** that feels real. Technology company Curiscope has created a **3-D** virtual reality experience about great white sharks. Viewers can watch digitally produced sharks that look real swim freely in the ocean. Landmark Entertainment Group is building a virtual reality theme park in China. It will include a virtual zoo and aquarium.

With live streams and virtual reality, viewers can watch live or digitally produced animals in their natural **habitats**. This is something people never could do in zoos or marine parks. More importantly, the wild animals are free instead of held in captivity.

TV channel Animal Planet has many live webcams of animals, including sloths! These videos show animals in the wild and in zoos to inspire viewers to value wildlife.

THE FUTURE OF ANIMAL CAPTIVITY

In recent years, the captive animal movement has sparked some changes. After the release of *Blackfish*, SeaWorld's profits dropped 84 percent in 2015. In 2016, the company announced it will phase out its theatrical orca performances. In 2017, SeaWorld opened a new exhibit featuring orcas' natural behavior. It includes live captive orcas alongside video footage of wild orcas.

However, while SeaWorld attendance is decreasing, zoos are growing in popularity. In 2016, many zoos had higher attendance than ever before. This rise in interest may be due to new designs and features in zoos. Most zoo exhibits use concrete elements. But some zoos have begun to build real landscapes that more closely resemble the wild **habitats** of their animals. These

Jörg Junhold is the director of Zoo Leipzig in Germany. The exhibits at this zoo are as close to natural habitats as possible.

landscapes feature natural plants and plenty of sunlight. They also allow more room for the animals to roam.

Experts believe zoos will continue to improve their exhibits in the future. Because of this, it is unlikely that zoos will be completely replaced. But animal **advocates** can still hold zoos to high standards. They will continue to fight for the welfare of captive animals!

TIMELINE

2500 BCE — The first menageries are created in Egypt and Mesopotamia.

1700s–1800s — The first public zoos open in Europe and the United States.

1907 — Animal trainer Carl Hagenbeck designs the first zoo without cages or fences.

1924 — The AZA is founded. It accredits zoos, aquariums, and marine parks based on certain standards.

1964 — SeaWorld opens in San Diego, California.

1995 — The Elephant Sanctuary is founded in Tennessee.

2013 — The popular film *Blackfish* is released and shifts public opinion of animal captivity.

2016 — SeaWorld stops breeding orcas in captivity and announces plans to end orca performances.

28

BECOME AN ANIMAL ADVOCATE

Do you want to become an advocate for captive animal rights? Here are some steps you can take today!

Spread the word. Education is key! Tell your family and friends about captive animal welfare.

Investigate. Research zoos and marine parks online before attending them. Find out if they are accredited and how they treat their animals.

Contact lawmakers. Contact your state's lawmakers and ask that laws protecting captive animals be improved.

Research organizations. Find an animal rights organization that is right for you. You can become a member, go to events, or sign up for newsletters!

GLOSSARY

accredit – to give official approval based on set standards. Something that meets set standards is accredited.

advocate – a person who defends or supports a cause.

aggressive (uh-GREH-sihv) – displaying hostility.

alternative – a choice from among two or more things.

confine – to hold or keep within a limited space.

controversial – relating to a discussion marked by strongly different views.

disaster – an event that causes damage, destruction, and often loss of life.

donate – to give. A donation is something that is given.

endangered – in danger of becoming extinct.

environment – surroundings, especially those that affect the growth and well-being of a living thing. *Environment* can also refer to nature and everything in it, such as the land, sea, and air.

ethics – rules of moral conduct followed by a person or group. Something that is unethical is morally wrong.

habitat – a place where a living thing is naturally found.

rehabilitate – to bring something back to a normal, healthy condition.

sanctuary – a refuge for wildlife where hunting is illegal.

stimulating – exciting to activity or growth.

technology (tehk-NAH-luh-jee) – machinery and equipment developed for practical purposes using scientific principles and engineering.

3-D – having length, width, and height. *3-D* stands for three-dimensional.

ONLINE RESOURCES

To learn more about captive animal welfare, visit **abdobooklinks.com**. These links are routinely monitored and updated to provide the most current information available.

INDEX

A
accreditation, 10, 11, 12
alternatives to animal captivity, 24, 25
Animal Welfare Act, 20
Association of Zoos and Aquariums, 10, 11

B
Blackfish, 19, 26

C
Canada, 8
captive breeding, 10, 12, 14, 19
China, 6, 25
circuses, 5, 7, 18
conservation, 10, 14, 15, 16, 17, 19, 24
Costa Rica, 21
Curiscope, 24, 25

D
donations, 10, 17, 19

E
education, 8, 14, 16
Egypt, 6
ethics, 5, 16, 17, 18
Explore.org, 24

F
Flipper, 12
France, 8

G
Germany, 9
Greece, 6

H
Hagenbeck, Carl, 9
history of animal captivity, 6, 7, 8, 9, 10, 12, 14, 18, 19, 20, 21, 26

I
India, 21
Italy, 6

L
Landmark Entertainment Group, 25
laws and regulations, 18, 20, 21, 22
London Zoo, 12
Los Angeles Zoo, 14

M
Marine Mammal Protection Act, 20
Marine Studios, 12

Ménagerie du Jardin des Plantes, 8
menageries, 6
Mesopotamia, 6
Mexico, 6
Montezuma, 6

P
People for the Ethical Treatment of Animals, 18

R
rehabilitation, 14, 15, 17

S
San Diego Wild Animal Park, 14
San Diego Zoo, 10
sanctuaries, 22, 24
sea pens, 22
Sealand of the Pacific, 19
SeaWorld, 12, 19, 26

T
technology, 5, 24, 25

U
United Kingdom, 8, 12, 21
United States, 8, 10, 11, 12, 14, 20, 21